Oh My Baby, Little One

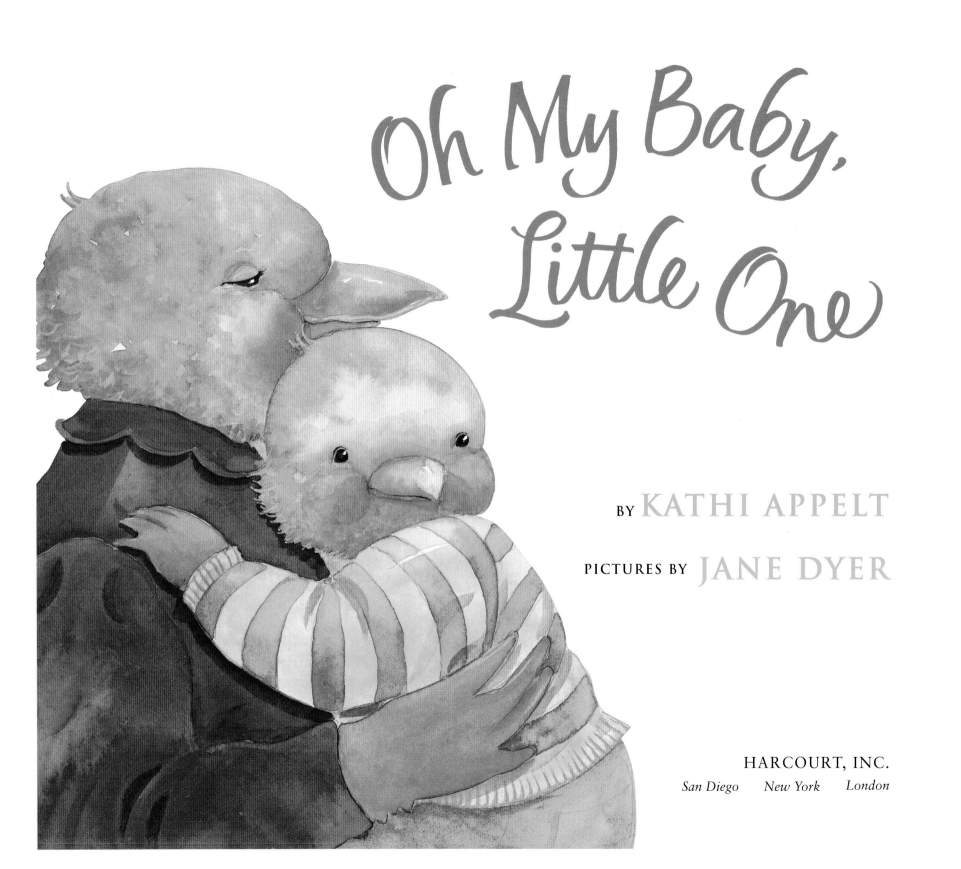

Oh My Baby, Little One

BY KATHI APPELT

PICTURES BY JANE DYER

HARCOURT, INC.

San Diego   New York   London

Library of Congress Cataloging-in-Publication Data
Appelt, Kathi, 1954–
Oh my baby, little one/Kathi Appelt; illustrated by Jane Dyer.
p. cm.
Summary: A mother explains to her child all the ways her love remains even while she's away.
[1. Mother and child—Fiction. 2. Love—Fiction. 3. Stories in rhyme.] I. Dyer, Jane, ill. II. Title.
PZ8.3.A554Oh 2000
[E]—dc21   99-6363
ISBN 0-15-200041-0

E F

Printed in Hong Kong

The illustrations in this book were painted in Windsor & Newton watercolors
on Arches 140 lb. hot-press watercolor paper.
The display type was hand-lettered by Judythe Sieck.
The text type was set in Sabon.
Color separations by Bright Arts Ltd., Hong Kong
Printed by South China Printing Company, Ltd., Hong Kong
This book was printed on totally chlorine-free Nymolla Matte Art paper.
Production supervision by Stanley Redfern and Pascha Gerlinger
Designed by Judythe Sieck

To Kacie, Bradley, and Debbie Leland,
with love —K. A.

To Allyn and Eamon —J. D.

Oh my baby, little one,
the hardest thing I do
is hold you tight, then let you go,
and walk away from you.

But even when I'm far away,
this love I have will stay
and wrap itself around you
every minute of the day.

So blow a kiss and wave good-bye–
my baby, don't you cry.
This love is always with you,
like the sun is with the sky.

It sits upon your shoulder
while you sing a happy song.
Clap your hands and tap your toes–
this love will sing along.

It nestles in your pocket
and makes itself so small
that when you're busy playing,
you won't notice it at all.

But still this love is with you,
like the leaves are with the trees,
like the sand is with the sandbox,
like the kite is with the breeze.

It slips inside your lunch box
and underneath your cap.
When your teacher reads a storybook,
it settles on your lap.

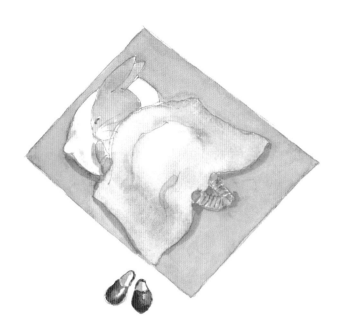

And when it's time to take a nap—
Shh, don't make a peep.
This love will curl up close to you
and keep watch while you sleep.

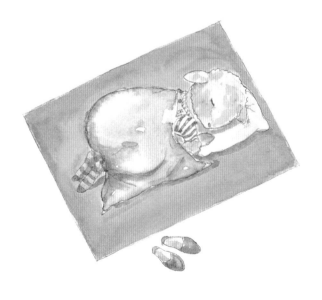

It snuggles on your pillow
and later on your sleeve.
Now stretch your fingers, rub your eyes—
this love will never leave.

It stays beside you always,
through everything you do.
And you might be surprised to know,
this love is with me, too.

It nestles in my collar
while I get my day's work done.
I hear it whisper in my ear,
My baby, little one.

It might hide inside my desk drawer
or slip inside my shoe,
but still, it's always with me—
it stays the whole day through.

It curls around my coffee cup
and perches on my chair.
It doesn't matter where I go,
this love is everywhere.

But oh my baby, little one,
the sweetest thing I do
is sweep you up and hold you tight
and come back home to you.